LEE

THE RABBIT WITH EPILEPSY

BY DEBORAH M. MOSS
ILLUSTRATED BY CAROL SCHWARTZ

WOODBINE
HOUSE

Lee and her Grandpa Jake were fishing on the river bank. They sat very still for such a long time that a butterfly landed on Lee's fishing pole. But the fish weren't biting.

Suddenly, Lee's fishing pole wiggled. It jerked and it jumped! Lee had a fish!

"Quick!" Grandpa shouted. "It's getting away!" But Lee didn't answer; just the tips of her ears twitched. "What's wrong—are you sleeping?" Grandpa shouted again. Lee's eyes were wide open, but she didn't even blink.

Then the fish pulled hard. It jumped in the air. That fish pulled Lee's fishing pole right into the water! Grandpa grabbed for the pole—a little too slowly. Then he tripped on a log and fell in the river. Splash!

When Grandpa climbed out again, spitting and sputtering, Lee was just sitting there, shaking with laughter. "Grandpa," Lee asked him, "what are you doing? You'll scare all the fish away, splashing like that."

At supper that evening, Grandpa Jake told Lee's parents how the big fish swam away with Lee's pole.
"What fish?" Lee asked, with a frown on her face. "What do you mean? I don't remember *anything.*"

Lee's father laughed and tickled her chin. "Don't be silly," he said, "you can tell us what happened. We aren't mad at you, Lee, for losing your pole."

But Lee didn't answer or even look at her dad. Just as before, she stared straight ahead.

A few moments later, Lee blinked and looked up. She smiled at her mother: "More carrot juice, please." Lee's mother and father and Grandfather Jake all looked at each other and scratched their heads. What was the matter with Lee?

The next morning, Lee's mom woke her early. She said, "Come along, Lee, let's go to the doctor. *He'll* tell us why you can't remember what happened yesterday down at the river."

In Dr. Bob's office, Lee sat on a table and Dr. Bob looked in her eyes and her throat. He tapped on her knees with a soft rubber hammer and asked Lee's parents all about her.

Then Dr. Bob said that he wanted to see what was going on inside Lee's brain. "I'll just paste some wires onto your head. It won't hurt a bit," Dr. Bob promised, "and the paste will come right off."

The paste on Lee's head felt sticky and cold, but Lee didn't mind it at all. She lay very still and looked at the ceiling, and soon Dr. Bob was through with the test.

"Am I okay?" Lee asked him. "What did my brain tell you?"
"Lee, you have epilepsy," Dr. Bob said. "Some people call it a seizure disorder."

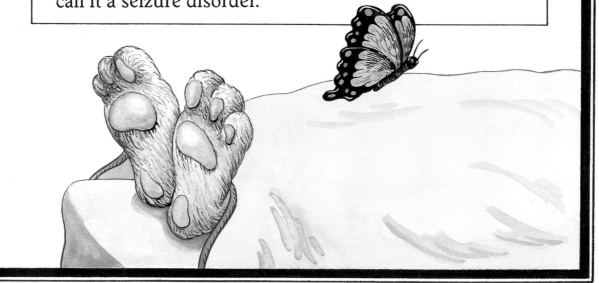

Dr. Bob laughed and gave Lee a hug. "No, Lee, when *you* have a seizure, you have a staring spell, just like you had at the river. Your eyes stay wide open, but you can't see, hear, or talk."

Dr. Bob went on. "There are different kinds of seizures, too. Some seizures make you fall down and shake all over. Some seizures make just one arm or a leg shake. And other seizures make everything look or sound strange to you for a moment."

Lee was too scared to ask any questions, but Dr. Bob explained. He said, "Your brain and your body are filled with millions of tiny cells like little batteries. Your brain cells send signals to the other parts of your body to tell them what to do."

"When you have epilepsy, your brain sometimes sends out mixed-up messages so you can't move, or think, or do things quite right for a little while. That's called having a seizure." Lee wrinkled her forehead. "I'm mixed up right now. Does that mean I'm having a seizure?"

Lee's eyes grew as round as the clock on the wall. "Will *I* have those kinds of seizures, too?" she asked.
Dr. Bob smiled. "I don't think so," he said. "But if you did, I could give you some medicine to help you."

Then Dr. Bob gave
Lee's mother some pills. He said, "Lee,
this medicine is especially for *your* kind of epilepsy.
If you take it everyday, it will help stop your seizures."
"Thank you," Lee told him, but she was still worried.
How could she do anything if she had seizures?

A couple of days passed and the weather got colder. Then Grandpa gave Lee a new fishing pole. "I can't use this," Lee said. "What if I lose it? I could have a seizure again."

But Grandfather wouldn't take "no" for an answer, and soon they were back at the river. They sat very still and whispered so softly, you could have heard a pine needle drop. But the fish weren't biting.

Suddenly, Grandpa's fishing pole wiggled. It jerked and it jumped. He had a fish! Lee looked at her Grandpa, but this time *he* was asleep. If she didn't act fast, the fish would escape!

Lee ran to her Grandpa and grabbed for his pole. She yelled and she shouted to wake him. Grandpa opened his eyes and let out a whistle, then they reeled in the fish together.

After they took the fish off the hook, Grandpa gave it to Lee to hold. "I knew you could do it," he said with a wink. "You can do *anything*."
Lee smiled and nodded and held up the fish. "You know what?" she said. "I *can*!"